Jean Lyons School of Music
228 - 1555 West 7th Avenue
Vancouver, B.C. V6J 1S1

Jean Lyons School of Music

Emily's
Eighteen Aunts

Story by Curtis Parkinson
Illustrated by Andrea Wayne von Königlsöw

Stoddart
Kids
TORONTO • NEW YORK

*To my Aunt Winnie,
who always had time for a small boy,
and to good-hearted relatives everywhere.
— C.P.*

*To my aunts, Ruth, Shirley, and Kaye, and to
my mother, Margaret, and my husband, Rainer.
— A. WvK.*

Published in Canada in 2002 by
Stoddart Kids,
a division of Stoddart Publishing Co. Limited
895 Don Mills Road, 400 ñ 2 Park Centre, Toronto, Ontario M3C 1W3

Published in the United States in 2002 by
Stoddart Kids
a division of Stoddart Publishing Co. Limited
PMB 128, 4500 Witmer Estates, Niagara Falls, New York 14305-1386

www.stoddartkids.com

To order Stoddart Kids books please contact General Distribution Services
In Canada Tel. (416) 213-1919 FAX (416) 213-1917
Email cservice@genpub.com
In the United States Toll-free tel. 1-800-805-1083 Toll-free FAX 1-800-481-6207
Email gdsinc@genpub.com

06 05 04 03 02 1 2 3 4 5

National Library of Canada Cataloguing in Publication data

Parkinson, Curtis
Emily's eighteen aunts

ISBN 0-7737-3336-1

I. Von Königslöw, Andrea Wayne II. Title.

PS8581.A76234E45 2002   jC813'.54   C2001-904216-7
PZ7.P23918Em 2002

*Emily advertises for an aunt and gets far more than she bargained for.
When her expectations are exceeded, she must come to terms with what to do
about eighteen eccentric aunts.*

THE CANADA COUNCIL | LE CONSEIL DES ARTS
FOR THE ARTS | DU CANADA
SINCE 1957 | DEPUIS 1957

*We acknowledge for their financial support of our
publishing program the Canada Council, the Ontario Arts
Council, and the Government of Canada through the
Book Publishing Industry Development Program (BPIDP).*

Printed and bound in Hong Kong, China by
Book Art Inc., Toronto

Sarah had an aunt who took her to the ballet.
Chris had grandparents who cheered at her baseball games.
James had an uncle who treated him to banana splits.

Emily didn't have anyone like that.

She had her mother, of course,
but her mother was busy looking after the new baby.

So, Emily printed an ad and tacked it up
on the supermarket notice board.

WANTED
AN AUNT FOR EMILY.
PLEASE APPLY SATURDAY AT
32 MAPLE STREET, APARTMENT 4

Saturday arrived.
All morning Emily watched from the window
of their small apartment.
No one came.

All afternoon she paced up and down.
Still no one came.

She was about to give up
when there was a knock at the door!
Emily ran to answer it.

"Hello, Emily, I could be your Aunt Winnie,"
said a neatly dressed, gray-haired lady.

Then, to Emily's surprise,
two more ladies popped up behind Aunt Winnie!

"And I could be your Aunt Roxie," said one.

"Your Aunt Carmen," said the other.

"Oh! Uh . . . please come in," Emily said.

No sooner had Emily shut the door
than she heard another knock.
This time she saw a *sea* of smiling women —
all wanting to be her aunts!

They marched right in.
They sat on the floor, leaned on the windowsills,
perched on the piano.

"Do you like ballet, Emily?" Aunt Winnie asked.

"Or baseball?" asked Aunt Roxie.

"And ice cream?" Aunt Carmen asked.

"Oh, yes!" Emily said. This was just what she had hoped for.

Emily's mother came in to see what all the fuss was about.

"These are my new aunts," said Emily proudly.

Her mother went a little wobbly,
but the aunts fanned her and made her tea.
Soon she felt better.

"We're from the Senior Center
down the street," Aunt Winnie explained.
"We'd love to take Emily to the ballet."

They filled two rows,
just behind Emily's friend
Sarah and her aunt.
Emily was thrilled with the
dancers, and so were the aunts.
All except Aunt Roxie,
who nodded off and dropped
her purse. Everything —
lipstick, eye liner, four dollars
and thirty cents in change, a
Frisbee, two cans of pop, and
an electric foot massager —
spilled out and rolled
down the aisle!

The prima ballerina was so
startled, she sailed right past
her partner! Emily sank down
in her seat as everyone,
including Sarah, turned to stare.

Afterward, Aunt Roxie said, "Sorry, Emily.
I guess ballet isn't for me. I love baseball, though."

"My team is playing next Saturday," Emily told her.

Surely, Emily thought,
nothing could go wrong at a baseball game.

The aunts all came.
They cheered lustily for Emily,
which gave her a warm feeling inside.

Then the umpire called Emily out
as she slid into second.

Aunt Carmen charged onto the field.
"Hey, Ump! You're as blind as a bat!" she shouted.
"Emily was safe. Safe by a mile!"

"Who is *that?*" asked Emily's friend Chris.

Emily cringed.
She watched the other aunts drag Aunt Carmen away.
If only they had just sat and cheered like everyone else!

The next Saturday,
Emily's eighteen aunts
suggested they go to an
ice cream parlor for a treat.
Before they had a chance
to order, Aunt Winnie's
pygmy hedgehog, Wilbur,
escaped from her pocket
and scampered across
the floor!

Customers leapt onto chairs.
Waiters dropped their trays.
Aunt Winnie chased Wilbur under a table —
the *very* table where James and his uncle
were eating banana splits.

The owner ejected Wilbur —
and the aunts — and Emily.
Emily blushed scarlet as she passed James.

"Sorry, Emily. Next time I'll leave Wilbur home,"
Aunt Winnie said. "How about a picnic next Saturday?"

Emily shifted her feet.
"Well . . . uh . . ." She stared at the sidewalk.
"I *think* I'm going to be busy."

"Oh," said the aunts forlornly.
They said goodbye and trudged away.
Emily sighed as she watched them go.
If only they weren't so . . . so . . . *different.*

A long time passed. Then one day, Emily noticed an ad on the supermarket notice board. It said:

WANTED
Niece or Nephew for Lonely Aunts.
Apply at Senior Center.
P.S. Must be willing to put up with all kinds of aunts.

Emily stared at the ad — especially the word "lonely".

Emily
was lost in thought
as she helped
with the groceries.

She put the ice
cream in the
cupboard, the
cereal in the freezer,
the lettuce in the
dishwasher. When she
was finished, she
squared her shoulders
and headed for the door.

The Senior Center was empty,
except for one person playing solitaire in the corner.
It was Aunt Winnie.
"Is it really you, Emily?" she cried when she looked up.
"Wait right here. I'll phone the others."

Soon Aunt Roxie
raced in from the beauty parlor,
followed by Aunt Carmen from the fitness center,
and Aunt Petunia from the park.
Other aunts began appearing, too.

"Hooray! Emily's back!" they cheered.
"Let's have a picnic tomorrow."

"Yes, let's!" said Emily.

The next day, Emily smiled as Aunt Carmen
fished her hat out of the duck pond,
Aunt Roxie played Frisbee with a few new friends,
Aunt Petunia shared cake with some Boy Scouts,
and Aunt Winnie and Wilbur played hide-and-seek.

Their picnic was definitely different from anyone else's.
Emily and her eighteen aunts wouldn't
have wanted it any other way.